PROPERTY OF
CITY LIBRARY

AND

....

To libraries and the librarians who ensure everyone can join in the story. – C.C.
To Denise, Sarah, Annie: some wonderful librarians. – J.J.

The artwork in this book was hand-drawn using digital brushes.

First published in 2022 by Floris Books. First published in the USA in 2023. Text © 2022 Caroline Crowe. Illustrations © 2022 John Joseph Caroline Crowe and John Joseph assert their right under the Copyright, Designs and Patents Act 1988 to be recognised as the Author and Illustrator of this Work. All rights reserved. No part of this book may be reproduced without prior permission of Floris Books, Edinburgh www.florisbooks.co.uk British Library CIP Data available. ISBN 978-178250-741-3 Printed in China by Leo Paper Products Ltd

Floris Books supports sustainable forest management by printing this book on materials made from wood that comes from responsible sources and reclaimed material

OUR INCREDIBLE
LIBRARY
BOOK

and the wonderful
journeys it took

OUR INCREDIBLE LIBRARY BOOK

and the wonderful journeys it took

WRITTEN BY
CAROLINE CROWE

ILLUSTRATED BY
JOHN JOSEPH

Floris
Books

Welcome to the library!

A room packed with stories, from ceiling to floor,
shelves of adventures for you to explore.

But each book has two stories – the tale the words tell,
and the tale of the journey it's been on as well...

Down there on the shelf, all tattered and worn,
is an old picture book; some pages are torn.

But once it was new, pages crisp, every one,
bursting with colours and brimming with fun.
It took pride of place on the new books display,
and was borrowed by Nia that very first day.

She took it straight home,
   and she read while she ate.
Even the broccoli
      went from her plate!

She bumped into doors,
   and she tripped on the rug.

Her favourite hot chocolate
went cold in the mug.
When she turned the last page,
she sat back with a smile.

It was hard to put back
on the book returns pile.

The book was the first
that Luis read himself.
He chose it from all of
the ones on the shelf.

He read to Abuela.
It made them both laugh.

He read it to Ana while she had her bath.

Hanna left it at Dad's. It was tricky to find,
crumpled up under Zig's giant behind.
They smoothed out the creases, except one or two.
It still had some wrinkles, but most good books do.

When Farhan felt sick, and all achy and hot,
he loved being read to: it helped him a lot.
It meant that he wasn't stuck there in his bed.
He was off and away on adventures instead.

For Zoe, the book was the
first in her house.
She hugged it to sleep, with
old Cheddar, her mouse.

She showed it to all of
the ducks at the park.

And read to the pigeons
until it got dark.

She borrowed more books
– Zoe borrowed A LOT –
But the first was the one
that she never forgot.

Miguel read it backwards, and then upside down.

Minnie and Vince read it wearing their crowns.

Wei read it with Tala, who read it with Tom.

He read it with Samir, and so it went on.

It got chewed by a dog.

It was soaked in the rain.

And then carried away in the doors of a train...

It was read by the fire,
first thing and at night,
with toasted marshmallows
in brilliant moonlight.

It grew dog-eared and dirty, and taped here and there.

But those marks told the tale of a book made to share.

Each reader gave life to
the tale of that book.

All the bedrooms it saw
and the journeys it took.

Whenever you take a book from the shelf,
seek out a good spot and enjoy it yourself...

You'll join in its tale and add to it too,
become part of its story, like all readers do.

OUR INCREDIBLE
LIBRARY
BOOK

and the wonderful
journeys it took

WRITTEN BY
CAROLINE CROWE

ILLUSTRATED BY
JOHN JOSEPH

BORROWED BY

Nia	
Luis	Tori
Hanna ☺	
Farhan	Riley
Zoe and Cheddar	LIAM
	Jin
	Noah
	Jayden
WET	

CAROLINE CROWE is an award-winning children's author from the UK. She was a newspaper journalist for many years, and can't believe she now gets to write children's stories as her job. Her picture books include *Pirates in Pyjamas*, *The Fairy Dogmother* and *How Do You Make a Rainbow?* She lives in Hampshire, England, with her young family, surrounded by chaos and their ever-growing book collection.

Our Incredible Library Book is inspired by Caroline's long-time fascination with the adventures of library books and the different meanings and memories they have for readers.

JOHN JOSEPH is a *New York Times*-bestselling illustrator whose books include *Chickens on the Loose*, *Dear Grandma*, *When Eleanor Roosevelt Learned to Jump a Horse* and the *Little Blue Truck* series. When he is not illustrating books, John teaches visual arts at a local elementary school. His students are a great inspiration, and they provide excellent critical feedback and suggestions for his books.

John grew up, and currently lives, along the front range of the Rocky Mountains in Colorado, where he can often be found playing with his two young boys and spending time at the public library.